Fox in Socks

By

Dr. Seuss

KU-479-973

7000341191179

HarperCollins *Children's Books*

™ & © Dr. Seuss Enterprises, L.P.
All rights reserved

A CIP catalogue record for this title is available from the British Library. No part of this publication
may be reproduced, stored in a retrieval system or transmitted in any form or by any means, electronic,
mechanical, photocopying, recording or otherwise, without the prior permission of HarperCollins
Publishers Ltd, 77-85 Fulham Palace Road, Hammersmith, London W6 8JB.

1 3 5 7 9 10 8 6 4 2

978-0-00-744155-6 (book only)
978-0-00-741423-9 (book & CD)

Fox in Socks
© 1963, 1991 by Dr. Seuss Enterprises, L.P.
All Rights Reserved
Published by arrangement with Random House Inc., New York, USA
First published in the UK in 1966
This edition published in the UK 2011 by HarperCollins Children's Books, a division
of HarperCollins Publishers Ltd, 77-85 Fulham Palace Road, London W6 8JB

www.harpercollins.co.uk

Printed and bound in China

Fox in Socks

Fox

Socks

Box

Knox

Knox in box.
Fox in socks.

Knox on fox
in socks in box.

Socks on Knox
and Knox in box.

Fox in socks
on box on Knox.

Chicks with bricks come.
Chicks with blocks come.
Chicks with bricks and
blocks and clocks come.

Look, sir. Look, sir.
Mr. Knox, sir.
Let's do tricks with
bricks and blocks, sir.
Let's do tricks with
chicks and clocks, sir.

First, I'll make a
quick trick brick stack.
Then I'll make a
quick trick block stack.

You can make a
quick trick chick stack.
You can make a
quick trick clock stack.

And here's a
new trick, Mr. Knox. . . .
Socks on chicks
and chicks on fox.
Fox on clocks
on bricks and blocks.
Bricks and blocks
on Knox on box.

Now we come to
ticks and tocks, sir.
Try to say this
Mr. Knox, sir. . . .

Clocks on fox tick.
Clocks on Knox tock.
Six sick bricks tick.
Six sick chicks tock.

Please, sir. I don't
like this trick, sir.
My tongue isn't
quick or slick, sir.
I get all those
ticks and clocks, sir,
mixed up with the
chicks and tocks, sir.
I can't do it, Mr. Fox, sir.

I'm so sorry,
Mr. Knox, sir.

Here's an easy
game to play.
Here's an easy
thing to say. . . .

New socks.
Two socks.
Whose socks?
Sue's socks.

Who sews whose socks?
Sue sews Sue's socks.

Who sees who sew
whose new socks, sir?
You see Sue sew
Sue's new socks, sir.

That's not easy,
Mr. Fox, sir.

Who comes? . . .
Crow comes.
Slow Joe Crow comes.

Who sews crow's clothes?
Sue sews crow's clothes.
Slow Joe Crow
sews whose clothes?
Sue's clothes.

Sue sews socks of
fox in socks now.

Slow Joe Crow sews
Knox in box now.

Sue sews rose
on Slow Joe Crow's clothes.
Fox sews hose
on Slow Joe Crow's nose.

Hose goes.
Rose grows.
Nose hose goes some.
Crow's rose grows some.

Mr. Fox!
I hate this game, sir.
This game makes
my tongue quite lame, sir.

Mr. Knox, sir,
what a shame, sir.

We'll find something
new to do now.
Here is lots of
new blue goo now.
New goo. Blue goo.
Gooey. Gooey.
Blue goo. New goo.
Gluey. Gluey.

Gooey goo
for chewy chewing!
That's what that
Goo-Goose is doing.
Do you choose to
chew goo, too, sir?
If, sir, you, sir,
choose to chew, sir,
with the Goo-Goose,
chew, sir. Do, sir.

Mr. Fox, sir,
I won't do it.
I can't say it.
I won't chew it.

Very well, sir.
Step this way.
We'll find another
game to play.

Bim comes.
Ben comes.
Bim brings Ben broom.
Ben brings Bim broom.

Ben bends Bim's broom.
Bim bends Ben's broom.
Bim's bends.
Ben's bends.
Ben's bent broom breaks.
Bim's bent broom breaks.

Ben's band. Bim's band.
Big bands. Pig bands.

Bim and Ben lead
bands with brooms.
Ben's band bangs
and Bim's band booms.

Pig band! Boom band!
Big band! Broom band!
My poor mouth can't
say that. No, sir.
My poor mouth is
much too slow, sir.

Well then . . .
bring your mouth this way.
I'll find it something
it can say.

Luke Luck likes lakes.
Luke's duck likes lakes.
Luke Luck licks lakes.
Luke's duck licks lakes.

Duck takes licks
in lakes Luke Luck likes.
Luke Luck takes licks
in lakes duck likes.

I can't blab
such blibber blubber!
My tongue isn't
made of rubber.

Mr. Knox. Now
come now. Come now.
You don't have to
be so dumb now. . . .

Try to say this,
Mr. Knox, please. . . .

Through three cheese trees
three free fleas flew.
While these fleas flew,
freezy breeze blew.
Freezy breeze made
these three trees freeze.
Freezy trees made
these trees' cheese freeze.
That's what made these
three free fleas sneeze.

Stop it! Stop it!
That's enough, sir.
I can't say
such silly stuff, sir.

Very well, then,
Mr. Knox, sir.

Let's have a little talk
about tweetle beetles. . . .

What do you know
about tweetle beetles?
Well . . .

When tweetle beetles fight,
it's called
a tweetle beetle battle.

And when they
battle in a puddle,
it's a tweetle
beetle puddle battle.

AND when tweetle beetles
battle with paddles in a puddle,
they call it a tweetle
beetle puddle paddle battle.
                    AND . . .

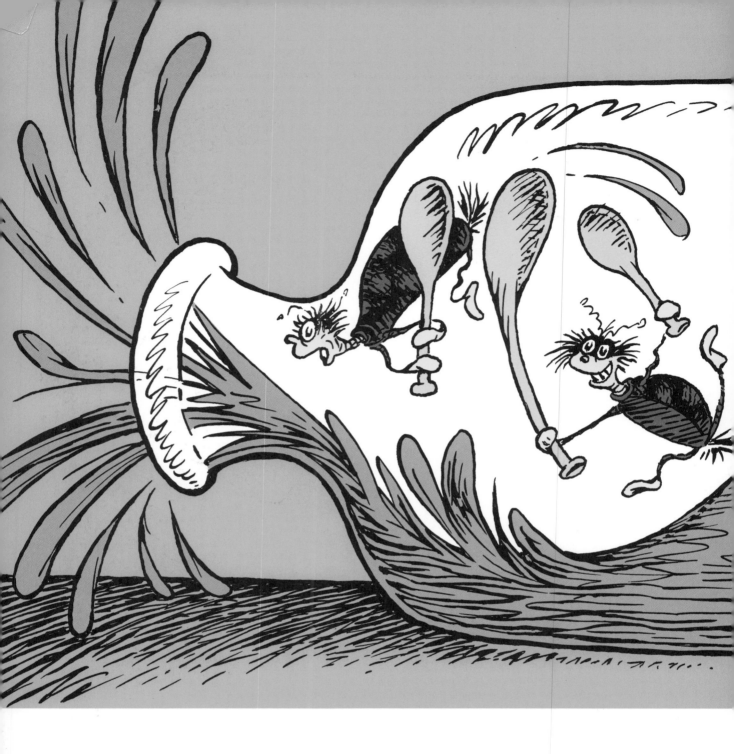

When beetles battle beetles
in a puddle paddle battle
and the beetle battle puddle
is a puddle in a bottle . . .

. . . they call this
a tweetle beetle
bottle puddle
paddle battle muddle.
AND . . .

When beetles
fight these battles
in a bottle
with their paddles
and the bottle's
on a poodle
and the poodle's
eating noodles . . .

. . . they call this
a muddle puddle
tweetle poodle
beetle noodle
bottle paddle battle.
AND . . .

Now wait
a minute,
Mr. Socks Fox!

When a fox is
in the bottle where
the tweetle beetles battle
with their paddles
in a puddle on a
noodle-eating poodle,
THIS is what they call . . .

. . . a tweetle beetle
noodle poodle bottled
paddled muddled duddled
fuddled wuddled
fox in socks, sir!

Fox in socks,
our game is done, sir.
Thank you for
a lot of fun, sir.

The Age of Castles

KNIGHTS AND CASTLES

Richard Dargie

700030807488

WAYLAND

WORCESTERSHIRE COUNTY COUNCIL	
748	
Bertrams	04.07.07
J941.03	£5.99
BV	

The Age of Castles

Titles in this series

CASTLE LIFE
CASTLE UNDER SIEGE
HOW CASTLES WERE BUILT
KNIGHTS AND CASTLES

Series editor: Alex Woolf
Editor: Jason Hook
Designer: Peter Laws
Cover Designers: Rachel Hamdi and Holly Fulbrook
Illustrator: Peter Dennis
Project artwork: John Yates
Picture Research: Carron Brown

Consultant: Richard Eales, Senior Lecturer in History, University of Kent.

First published in 1998 by Wayland Publisher Ltd
This edition revised in 2007 by Wayland,
an imprint by Hachette Children's Books.

© Copyright 1998 Wayland
All rights reserved

British Library Cataloguing in Publication Data
Dargie, Richard
Knights and castles. - (The age of castles)
1. Knights and knighthood - Juvenile literature
2. Castles - History - Juvenile literature
3. Middle Ages - Juvenile literature
I. Title
725.1'8'0902

ISBN 978 0 7502 5202 7
Printed and bound in China
Hachette Children's Books 338 Euston Road, London NW1 3BH

PICTURE ACKNOWLEDGEMENTS
The publishers wish to thank the following for permission to publish their pictures: (t=top;
c=centre; b=bottom; l=left; r=right) AKG London 9b, 27r, 29t, 36, 37; Bridgeman Art
Library, London/New York, /Bibliothèque Nationale, Paris 7t, 21t, 22, 30, 31t, /Bargello,
Florence 7bl, /British Library, London 9t, 17r, 41t, /Pinacoteca di Brera, Milan 17l, /British
Museum, London 31b, /Private Collection 41b; British Library, London 7r, 11t, 14; British
Museum 12, 23bl, 23br, 28, 29b, 38; © Bodleian Library, University of Oxford, 1998,
MS.Bodley 264, part 1, 12, 102, 24; Dean and Chapter, Durham University 15tl; E.T.
Archive 5, 8, 15r, 34, 42; Image Bank 18; Robert Harding 6; Stockmarket 23t; The Board
and Trustees of the Armouries IX.915, IX,1081, 25, IV.411, 33; The Master and Fellows of
Corpus Christi College, Cambridge 19b; Topham 35, 43; Wayland Picture Library 16;
Werner Forman Archive 39.